For Auntie Pat, and in memory of my dad, Barry—

family far away but close in my heart —T.S.

For Pender Island, north and south — A.A.

Text copyright © 2021 by Tiffany Stone
Illustrations copyright © 2021 by Ashlyn Anstee

21 22 23 24 25   5 4 3 2 1

Greystone Kids / Greystone Books Ltd.
greystonebooks.com

Cataloguing data available from Library and Archives Canada
ISBN 978-1-77164-620-8 (cloth)
ISBN 978-1-77164-621-5 (epub)

Editing by Kallie George
Copy editing by Elizabeth McLean
Proofreading by Doeun Rivendell
Jacket and text design by Sara Gillingham Studio
The illustrations in this book were rendered in a combination of gouache, crayons, and Adobe Photoshop.
Printed and bound in China by 1010 Printing International Ltd.

A special thanks to Dr. Marie Noël for her valuable contribution in reviewing this book.

Greystone Books gratefully acknowledges the Musqueam, Squamish, and Tsleil-Waututh peoples
on whose land our office is located.

Greystone Books thanks the Canada Council for the Arts, the British Columbia Arts Council,
the Province of British Columbia through the Book Publishing Tax Credit, and the Government of Canada
for supporting our publishing activities.

Little Narwhal, Not Alone

BY Tiffany Stone

ILLUSTRATED BY Ashlyn Anstee

GREYSTONE KIDS

GREYSTONE BOOKS · VANCOUVER/BERKELEY

Narwhal loves his frozen home.

But little narwhal longs to roam,

to see the sea beyond this ice,
Past polar bears, to brand-new sights.

And so while others hunt and play,
narwhal sets off on his way.

Narwhal swims by schools of fish: arctic char and cod.

SWISH SWISH!

A sassy seal sees whale and winks.
Drifting sea ice scrapes and clinks.

While way up in the Northern sky,
circling seabirds play I Spy.

On land stand two caribou.
And, there, ahead . . .

That view is new!

Brand-new sights
and brand-new sounds.

Narwhal's found
a new playground.

WHEEEEEEEEEEEEEEE!

A perfect place to share.

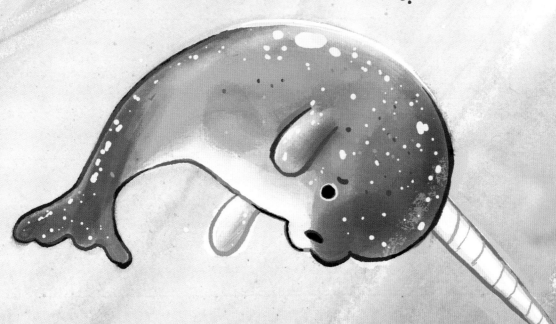

Except there are
no narwhals there . . .

So off to find some friends to play.
But narwhal can't decide which way.

Till . . .

PRRRRRRRRRRRRRRRRRRRRRRRRRRRRRRRRRRRRRR!

A new noise beckons him.
Narwhal picks that way to swim.

Certain it's a friendly stranger,
narwhal nears, discovers . . .

Quick, escape, without a peep!
Little narwhal dives

down

D
E
E
P

He swims . . .

. . . and swims . . .

. . . and swims some more.

His flippers ache.
His fluke is sore.

P'fffffffwaaaaaa!

P'fffffffwaaaaaa!

Then up, up, up from murky depths,
he surfaces and takes deep breaths.

More careful now, he spends each day
in search of narwhals, mottled gray.

But far off from his frozen home,
little narwhal's all alone.

spouting spray
and splashing tails.

No, not ice.
They're ice-white whales,

They look like him— or close enough—

though no one sports a twisty tusk.

Narwhal nears to say hello.

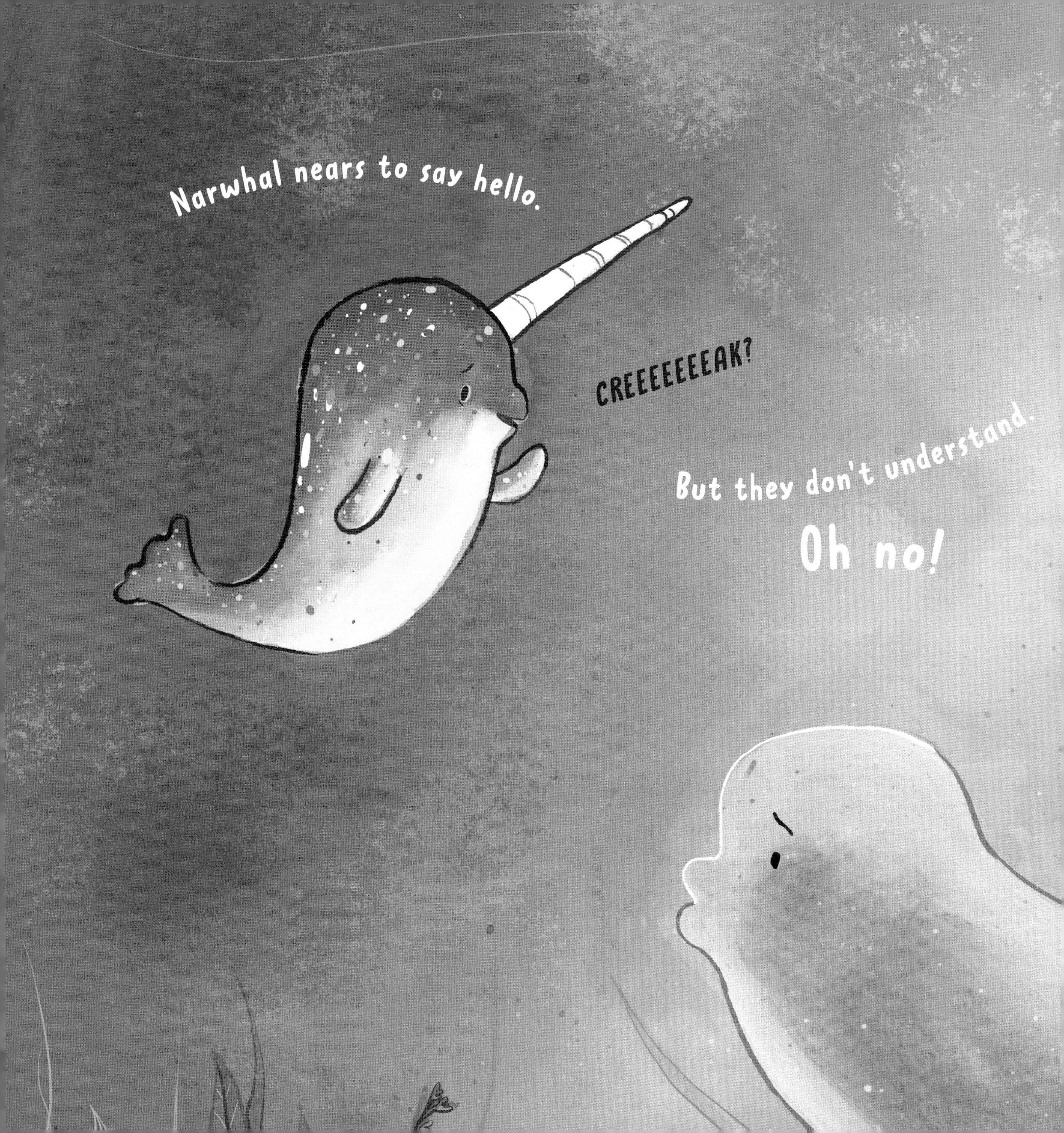

But they don't understand.

Oh no!

Still, narwhal tries hard not to care.

He's sure there's something that they share.

So when the pod starts moving on,

little narwhal tags along.

CHIRRRRRRP!

The whales sing as they go . . .
a song that narwhal doesn't know.

And when it's time to
hunt for food . . .

he doesn't eat the fish they do.

Too many things are not the same.
Narwhal feels alone again.

He's just about to slip away,

when . . .

...all the whales begin to play.

Although a lot is not the same, narwhal knows he knows this game!

Flippers splish. He joins right in.

And . . .

SQUIRT

. . . the new whales welcome him!

They frisk in groups of
four, three, two—

games he knows . . .
Then something new.

BLOOP!

Narwhal tries . . .
. . . and tries again.

He just . . . can't . . . do it . . . right . . .

And then . . .

Little narwhal loves to roam,
and now he won't be all alone.

He'll see new sights and hear new sounds
with all his new friends gathered round.

A TRUE STORY

This story is based on the unlikely real-life friendship between two different species of whales. A young narwhal, most distinguishable by his tusk (which is actually a long protruding tooth!), was spotted in the St. Lawrence River estuary in Quebec, Canada, among a group of young belugas four years in a row. The narwhal appears to have wandered more than 600 miles (1000 kilometers) away from his home in the Arctic. It is not unusual for young narwhals to wander, but this is just too far for him to find his way home or meet up with other members of his species. Although they are distantly related, beluga whales and narwhals usually do not interact. However, to everyone's surprise, it looks like the young narwhal may have been adopted by the group of young belugas. Now, the narwhal has even been observed blowing bubbles from time to time, just like his beluga cousins!

What else will he learn? Will he try to blow rings in the water or try to make some new sounds that his cousins are experts at? Will the belugas pick up any behaviors from him? Every summer, researchers keep an eye on the whales of the St. Lawrence and this remarkable friendship.

— Marie Noël, PhD, marine biologist